ANGELA'S WINGS

Eric Jon Nones

FARRAR STRAUS GIROUX

NEW YORK

CALLAHAN LIBRARY
ST. JOSEPH'S COLLEGE
25 Audubon Avenue
Patchogue, NY 11772-2399

Copyright © 1995 by Eric Jon Nones

All rights reserved

Published simultaneously in Canada by HarperCollins Canada Ltd

Printed and bound in the United States of America by Berryville Graphics

Designed by Filomena Tuosto

The Underdog character copyright © 1995 Leonardo—T.T.V.

Reprinted by permission of Filmtel International Corporation

First edition, 1995

Library of Congress Cataloging-in-Publication Data

Nones, Eric Jon.

Angela's wings / Eric Jon Nones—1st ed.

p.   cm.

[1. Wings—Fiction.] I. Title.

PZ7.N7315An 1995 [E]—dc20 94-30321 CIP AC

For Stephen Roxburgh,
who saw my wings and gave me the sky

Angela woke up one day and discovered
she had sprouted wings.
"Oh, terrific, what am I supposed to do
with these things?" She hoped maybe no
one would notice.

They noticed.

"For heaven's sake, where on earth did those come from?" her dad asked.

"How should I know!" Angela answered back.

"She must have gotten them from your side
of the family," Angela's mom told her dad.
"Cool," her little brother added.
"Think they'll attract attention?"

Did they ever! When Angela went outside,
everyone laughed and everyone made jokes,
and Angela tried hard not to let it get her
down. But it wasn't easy.

"I knew a guy in Toledo, most beautiful set of wings I ever saw," said the janitor in Angela's building. "He didn't do much with 'em, though—a real pity. Such a waste."

"Hey, Angela, where you hidin'? Off laying an egg or somethin'?"

"Leave her alone. So Angela has wings, Bernie DeNunzio has a big nose, so what."

"Why, I remember a lady friend of mine with six fingers on each hand and she played the piano like a dream," Angela's grandmother told her. "Everyone's got something special, child. Just depends on what you do with it, that's all."

So Angela started doing all the things she
used to do.
  She went to the same places.

Played the same games.
And before she realized it, Angela was
having more fun than she'd ever had.

Not to mention what a hit she was at the
St. Bartholomew's Christmas pageant!

And as the months flew by, Angela's life
had gone back to normal.
Well, sort of. People still did notice her.

And there was no denying she did stick out in a crowd.
All in all, things were pretty different.

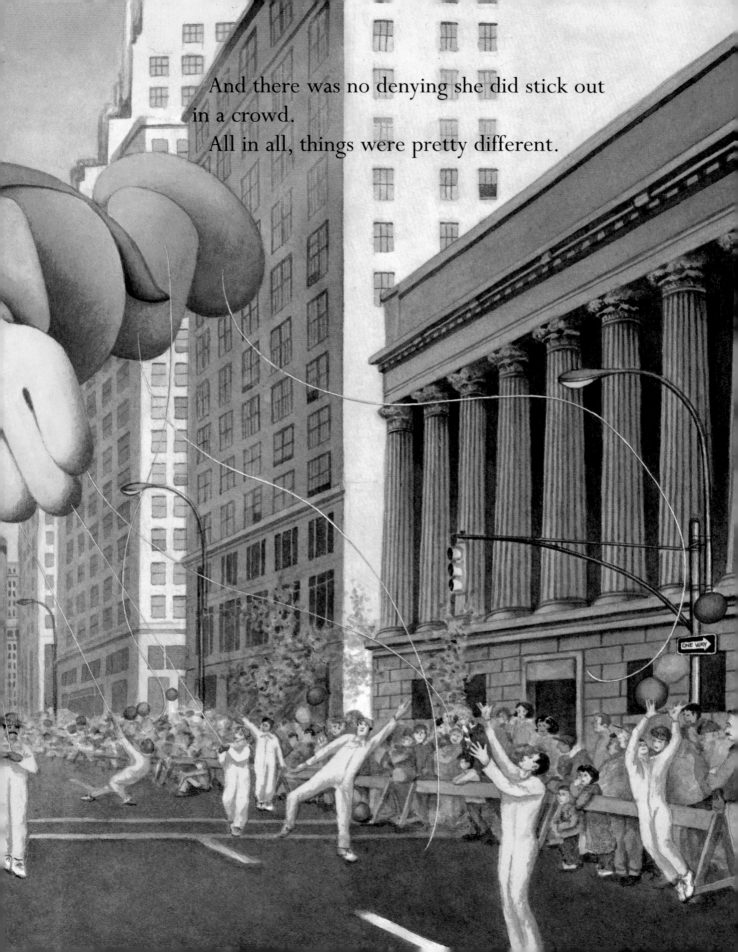

But Angela had discovered she liked that.

ST. JOSEPH'S COLLEGE CALLAHAN LIBRARY

3 1960 01425 23

JUN Gr.K-3
Ch. Fiction
Nones, Eric Jon.

Angela's Wings